PRINCESSES ON THE RUN

ON THE

RUN

by smiljana coh

RP|KIDS
PHILADELPHIA · LONDON

© 2013 by Smiljana Coh

All rights reserved under the Pan-American and International Copyright Conventions

Printed in China

*This book may not be reproduced in whole or in part, in any form or by any means,
electronic or mechanical, including photocopying, recording, or by any information storage and
retrieval system now known or hereafter invented, without written permission from the publisher.*

Books published by Running Press are available at special discounts for bulk purchases in the United States
by corporations, institutions, and other organizations. For more information, please contact the
Special Markets Department at the Perseus Books Group, 2300 Chestnut Street, Suite 200, Philadelphia,
PA 19103, or call (800) 810-4145, ext. 5000, or e-mail special.markets@perseusbooks.com.

ISBN 978-0-7624-4612-4

Library of Congress Control Number: 2012946109

9 8 7 6 5 4 3 2 1
Digit on the right indicates the number of this printing

Designed by Ryan Hayes and Frances J. Soo Ping Chow
Edited by Marlo Scrimizzi
Typography: Caligula Dodgy, Mr Moustache, and Old Standard

Published by Running Press Kids
An Imprint of Running Press Book Publishers
A Member of the Perseus Books Group

2300 Chestnut Street
Philadelphia, PA 19103–4371

Visit us on the web!
www.runningpress.com

To my husband, Fabio, Crvenkapica,
Marlo, and Kirsten

Once upon a time there lived
a beautiful princess named Antonia.

She had the most
elegant dresses,

played with
the newest toys,

and had the largest book
collection in the entire kingdom.

But for a reason she could not quite pinpoint, she felt bored.

Antonia also had many friends,
but they were never available for play dates.

Cinderella was always
busy cleaning....

Rapunzel never left
her tower....

Snow White constantly had
her hands full....

And Sleeping Beauty was
always too tired.

As each day turned into night, which then turned into day,
Antonia grew more and more restless.

To cheer her up, Antonia's parents offered her more presents.
They gave her more dresses, more toys, and more books. A fish, a cat,
a dog, fancier dresses, a state-of-the-art computer, an elephant!

But Antonia was still bored.

As she stood in her bedroom surrounded by all her presents, Antonia began to feel lonely.

But what can I do? she asked herself.

Antonia felt a bolt of lightning go through her,
and she ran straight out of her room!

She ran out of the castle, through the town,
and straight into the deep dark forest. With every step she took,
she ran faster, and her heart beat more quickly.

Antonia didn't recognize this new feeling in herself.
Might this be the thing called "freedom" she had read about?

Antonia ran and ran until something long and soft
brushed into her face. Looking up, she realized
it was Rapunzel's long braid.

Rapunzel, who had been trapped in her tower
long enough, was also escaping!

The two princesses clasped hands and ran through the forest,
not thinking about what they had left behind.

Antonia and Rapunzel ran and ran—
but stopped when they heard a noise.

"Ouch!" squealed a voice.

Someone was hopping toward them wearing
a shiny glass slipper. It was Cinderella!

"Take that shoe off and come with us!"
Antonia told her, to which Cinderella happily agreed.

Antonia, Rapunzel, and Cinderella giggled and clapped
as they ran and ran as fast as they could.

When the three princesses reached a clearing, they found someone
hanging seven hats to dry. It was Snow White!

"Drop those and come with us!" Antonia told her.

She didn't have to tell her twice. Snow White kicked the clothes basket aside and quickly joined the run with her friends.

The four princesses couldn't contain their excitement and cheered and laughed as they continued onward.

"What on earth?" Sleeping Beauty said as she looked out her window. It had been years since she'd risen from her bed, but the laughter and cheers were enough to wake her from her deep sleep.

"Join us!" the group called out to her.

The five princesses were off,
running and skipping and ready to—

"Wait for me!" called Little Red Riding Hood.
She was on her way to her grandmother's house when she heard
all the excitement. Now was her chance to run away!

But Little Red Riding Hood wasn't the only one
who heard the princesses on the run. . . .

Bears, deer, rabbits, and all sorts of forest creatures
began crawling out to join the fun.

Soon even the Three Billy Goats Gruff
had joined the procession!

Suddenly everyone came to a stop. They reached the sea,
and there was nowhere else to go.

"What are we going to do now?" Little Red
Riding Hood wondered aloud.

Antonia looked at the beautiful sunset. This was the best day she'd ever had, and she had at last found her friends.

Maybe things could be different . . . ,
Antonia thought to herself. She was no longer bored.

"I should be getting home," Antonia answered at last.

The others scratched their heads and thought about this.
After all, who was going to tuck them into bed? So they nodded
in agreement and took Antonia's lead.

As everyone turned back toward their own castles and burrows,
the princesses and their woodland friends
chatted happily among themselves.

"Yes, we totally should do this again!"
Snow White told the shy deer at her side.

Antonia and her princess friends linked arms as they skipped home.
They were happy to return and sang songs about their future . . .

. . . all except for Sleeping Beauty,
who hadn't had this much excitement in a very long time.

And when the princesses returned, everything *was* different.

Rapunzel cut her hair into a much easier-to-manage bob. Her new 'do was so popular that girls from far and wide lined up to get their hair cut.

Cinderella designed a funky new dress, and she became
the envy of the entire castle. Soon she was trading
her fresh designs for help with her chores.

Sleeping Beauty discovered yoga. Suddenly she had
way more energy than she knew what to do with!

And Snow White could not stop running.
She felt sure she could go farther, so she ran a cross-country tour!

Antonia also felt refreshed after her run. She planned more play dates with her friends, and decided to donate her old toys, clothes, and books.

While doing this, she saw how incredibly lucky she was. Her very own elephant! Antonia had never before realized how special that was.

And when she wondered if her elephant liked to run too, Antonia
decided there was only one way to find out....

The End